Confession is a work of fiction. represent any particular perso establishments or organizatio are products of the author's imagination and are used fictitiously to give this book a sense of reality and authenticity. Ant resemblances of fictionalized event or incidents that involve real persons are purely coincidental.

Books purchased with a dull or missing cover are most likely stolen and unauthorized by the publisher. Please notify the publisher immediately of where and when you purchase the illegal copy.

Purple Publication
P.O. Box 1986
Pine Bluff, Arkansas 71613-1986

ISBN: **1479335894**
ISBN-13: 978-1479335893

Copyright © 2012 Cleopatra Kaine
All rights reserved.

The reproduction, transmission, utilization of this work in any whole or in part in any form by electronic, mechanical or other means now known or hereafter invented, including xerography, photocopy and recording or in any information storage or retrieval system is forbidden without written permission in writing from the copyright owner.

Printed in the United States of America

CONTENTS

Short Stories	Page
When a is Fed	5
Sunday Evening	14
Endless Love	23
Caught Up	45
Wedding Day	57
The Loner	73
Baby Daddy Drama	79
Halloween Massacre	86

Confession
A collection of short stories
Written by: Cleopatra Kaine

Ck

When a Woman is Fed up

June 16, 1999 is a day that Alexandria Jackson will always remember. That was the she got fed up with the bull shit that her husband was dishing out to her. It was a typical Wednesday morning. She got up at 6 o'clock. She woke her husband, Tony, up. He would get into the shower while she checks on the girls, who were babies at this time. Then she would cook breakfast for Tony. Alexandria was feeling kind on nauseated from the aroma of her cooking. She walked over to the trash can and relieved herself. She took the trash out before Tony came out the bathroom. He came in the kitchen with his purple and black wind suit on. He walked up to Alexandria and kissed her on the cheek. He poured himself a glass of OJ and sat at the table while Alexander continues to cook his breakfast. When she finished, she served Tony.

"Good morning love," she said every morning for the last three years.

Three years ago, Alexandria was graduating from

college with her bachelor of science in elementary education. Tony had just gotten draft in the NBA to the Lakers. They got married soon after. When the basketball season started, she started seeing less and less of him. Tony wanted Alexandria to stay at home and support him at the games. It wasn't until the first home game that Tony injury himself. It was the third quarter when he jumped up to assist and blew out his knee. The doctor said that he would not be able to play on it any more. All his dreams shattered. Tony sat the rest of the season on the sideline.

The Lakers gave him a job the next season as a trainer. He spends his days at the gym and come home late at night. One night, Tony came home late. Alexandria put Tony's dinner in the refrigerator. She left a note that his meal was in the frig. He came home and saw the note. He went upstairs and dragged Alexandria out the bed by her long black hair. He dragged all the way down the stairs. He shoved her to the refrigerator. "I want my dinner warm when I get home," he shouted. That is the first time he had every abuses to her. At that time, Alexandria was six months pregnant with their first daughter, Antonia. The next day, Tony went out and bought her roses.

The next year, Alexandria found out that she was pregnant again with their second daughter. This time, Alexandria decides to leave Tony. She packed up all her and Antonia stuff and left. She went to her mother house in Chicago. She stayed there two weeks before Tony came to get them. He promised Alexandria and her mother that he would not hit her again. Alexandria went back to LA with him. Soon as she put Antonia to bed, she went into the living room were Tony was sitting. He slapped her down to the ground. "That is for leaving me," he shouted. Alexandria cried, "I'm pregnant!" He looked at her as she got up of the floor. Tony slapped her back down on the floor. "I don't care if you are dying from cancer," he shouted. He went to the bar and grabs the bottle of Crown. He poured him a drink in a glass. "Who do you think told me where you were at?" He said as he took a sip from the glass. Alexandria looked at him in disbelief. She couldn't believe that her own mother would sell her out. "I bought that bitch a house and give her money every month," he said. "You will never get away from me." He threw the rest of the Crown on her. Then he got on top of her and had his way. Tears dropped from her eyes with each stroke. She cried, "Please stop!" He pushed harder into her. Then he releases himself into her. She lay on the floor and cried. He got up and went to the bathroom. These abuses continue until she had Alexis. Alexis was born a month before time.

      June 16, 1999 is a date that has been planned for a month now. She found out a month ago that she was pregnant for the third time and that she needed to take it easy because she had not fully healed from the second baby. So she decided to run to the only people that she trusts in the world, her best friends. She had known them all her adult life and lost contact with them when she married Tony. Marquelia Andies was shock to hear from Alexandria after all these years. Alexandria explained to Marquelia why she haven't been in contact with her and told Marquelia her problem. Marquelia agree to help Alexandria. Marquelia set up a name change for Alexandria and the kids. Alexandria went to the bank and withdrew $5000. The next week Marquelia came down and helped her set the leave, as they called it, up. They set the date and Marquelia went back home. Between that time and now, Alexandria was packing the SUV up with everything that she thought that was important. So today is the day that Alexandria Nicole Washington-Jackson will die forever. She is leaving hell for good. Or shall we say for now.

    Tony sat at the table and ate his morning breakfast. Alexandria went to the frig to get a bottle water. Tony looked at her. He notices that she didn't look well.

    "Are you alright? If you are not, you need to get away from me and I'll get a sitter for the girls."

    "Nothing is wrong with me," Alexandria said. She

didn't need for him to find out that she is pregnant again.

"Lex," Tony said, "I'm going to be late. I have to work overtime with one of the player. Where are the kids?"

"Still sleep," Alexandria said.

Tony finished eating his breakfast. He got up and put his dishes in the dishwasher. He grabbed his bag. He walked over to Alexandria and kissed her on the cheek.

"I love you, Lex," he said. "I'll call you later on today."

Tony walked out the back door and went to his Explore. Alexandria watches him as he drove off. She ran to the bathroom and stood on stop of the toilet. She pushes on a square on the ceiling and pulled out a purse with some very important document and a lot of money. Then went to the closest and pulled out some suitcases that Tony thought was empty. She put the suitcases in the car. She went back and took a shower and put on some clothes. Then she got the girls ready. At this time, the girls were one years and six months old. She put them in the car sit and locked the door. She started the car up and drove off. Antonia and Alexis went back to sleep. She went to a pawn shop. The man looked at the ring and thought that it was hot. She assured him that it wasn't hot. He gave her $500 for the ring. She hurried back to the car and took off. She went to a parking garage. Alexandria went to the fifth deck and park next to a black Expedition. She took everything out of the car. She put the girls in the truck and put in a cartoon DVD for them to watch. She took all her money, which was in cash, and personal items out of the purse. She threw the purse in the front seat of the Lexus. Alexandria knew he had a tracker put in that purse. She threw the cell phone and keys in the driver seat of the Lexus. She got into the truck and looked in the glove compartment. In it was her new id with her children new birth certificate.

"Now I will be known as Tara Morris," Alexandria said.

Alexandria started the truck and drove off.

Later on that day, Tony decides to call home. When he didn't get an answer, he called her cell phone. When Alexandria didn't answer, he ran out the gym to the truck. He raced to his house. He opens the door. "Alexandria!" he shouted. There was no answer. He ran to the girls' room. They were nowhere to be found. He looked and notice that all the pampers they had bought last night were gone. He ran to the room and looked in the closet. He saw that the two blue suit cases that have been sitting in the closet were gone. He went to his office in the house and pulled out his laptop. He pulled up the tract device that he put on Alexandria's car. He found her at the parking garage at 124th and Lexon. He rushed out the house into his truck. He drove off to the garage. He searched the garage and found the Lexus. "I'm going to beat this bitch ass when I see her," he said. He parked next to the car and got out. He opens her car with the key that he had. He heard a beep. He looked in the seat. He saw Alexandria's phone in the driver seat. He saw her purse that he put the tracking device in on the passenger side of the car. He looked in her phone to see who have she been calling. All he saw was his number. He slammed the door of the car.

"That bitch thinks she got away from me," he said. "I will find her."

Tony got into the truck and left.

Sunday Evening

That normal Sunday evening is an event for the sisters at St. Mark Missionary Baptist Church. Rev. Dobson preached a great sermon. The sisters of the church listened to his every word. The deacons hummed and the mothers shouted amen. Hand fan was going back and forth. Sister Nellie, the church organist, played as Rev. Dobson sermon rose to a climax. The big man in the choir stand was rocking himself to sleep while the other was trying not to snore. But most of the sisters in the church were looking at the youth minister behind Rev. Dobson. His name is Jorrie Keller.

Jorrie Keller wasn't your usual minster. He stood about 6'3. His coco brown skin brings out his doggy brown eyes. He is husky. The shirts he wore shows of the cuts of his abs. His gold tee was neatly trimmed and he has a bald head. He is about 26 or 27. That didn't matter to the sister of the congregation. The thing that they cared about the most was that he was single. He has a degree and making his own money. That's all the qualification that Jorrie needed.

Jorrie drove the church van. When he started driving the van, there was a lot of empty sits. He has been driving the van for about a year now and he have to make two trips to the church to take everyone home. His first load consisted of the older people (mother of the church, deacons and elderly.) The second load consisted of women. They ranged from the age 21 to 50. All of these women were single, divorce or widow. They were trying their best to take Jorrie home. They wanted to be Mrs. Jorrie Keller.

On one Sunday, everything went as usual. The choir sang songs of joy. The ushers passed the money basket around and Rev. Dobson presented the congregation with a great sermon. After church, everyone gathered around the church van. Rev. Dobson stood outside and observed the crowd around the church van. As people got into the van he notices none of the young women was boarding the van. He walked over and grabbed Mother Walker. Mother Walker was stalled by the pastor. She smiled at him and hugged him with warm greetings.

"Pastor," Mother Walker said, "that was a great sermon."

"Thank you," Rev. Dobson said.

Jorrie looked over to call Mother Walker. Rev. Dobson waved his hand to go on. Jorrie asked one of the other sisters in that rode the van do they want to go home now. They looked at one another. Then finally, Sister Becca Benn got on the van and smiled. The other sister started to whisper. How dare she? One of the sisters said. Sister Benn hopped in the front seat of the van. Jorrie drove off.

"Drive carefully," Rev. Dobson said and smiled at Jorrie as he drove off.

Jorrie started dropping off the passengers one by one. He helped all off them off the van and made sure that they got into their homes. He was down to the last three sisters and Mother Walker. The whole time Mother Walker was on the van, she talked to Jorrie. The other sisters got kind of jealous because they usually talk to him. He decided that he was going to take Mother Walker home first.

Two of the three sisters were looking at each other meanly. If they said a word to one another, blows would have broken out between the two of them. They sat there looking at each other with the evil eye. One of them was a tall obese young lady. Her complication was very dark. Her eyes were bitty, very bitty. But she thought that she was the bomb. Her hair was braided. Her name was Meagan Miller. A lot of people like to call her MeMe. The other woman was an older woman. She looked as if she was only 41. Her skin was fair. Her hair was long and black that she wore pin back in a ball. She was a short woman. Not very heavy like people would think a woman her age should be. She sat up proud and with pride. Something her mother taught her when she was younger. She always wears her Sunday best. Ethel Washington was on the van with a tight grip on her bible. Jorrie looked back and saw the two staring at each other. He turns the music up loud. He thought that it might have calmed them down.

When Jorrie pulled up to Mother Walker's house, he got out to assist her. He walked her to the house. In the van, MeMe and her friend, Jamica Griffin, was talking. Ethel sat in the van quietly.

"I see you and Jorrie have been spending a lot of time together," said Jamica.

"Yes." said MeMe. "We're dating."

Ethel stared at MeMe in shock. MeMe smiled.

"Have yal done anything yet?" Jamica asked.

"A lady never tells," MeMe replied smiling.

They knew that Ethel was mad. Ethel was biting her bottom lip. *How dare he*, Ethel thinks to herself. After all I have done for him. Jorrie came back in the van and saw Ethel beautiful brown eyes almost go into tears. MeMe and Jamica smiled.

"What's wrong, Ethel?" Jorrie asked.

Ethel did not reply. She just bit her bottom lip even harder. MeMe giggled. Jorrie looked at her meanly.

He started the van and drove off. He took Jamica home first. Then it was the three of them. MeMe was still smiling. She thought that she had got rid of the only woman that stood between her and her dream man. Jorrie dropped MeMe off at her house. MeMe was expecting Jorrie to get out the van and open the door for her as he does every Sunday. But this time he didn't do it. MeMe smile turn into a frown as she walked away from the van. Then he drop Ethel off. He took the van back to the church. Rev. Dobson was waiting at the church. Jorrie got out the van. He walked toward the black sports car. Rev. Dobson rolled down his window.

"How was the ride?" he asked.

"Just fine," Jorrie answered.

"I know it was not just fine," Rev. Dobson said.

"Mother Walker called me and told me that you couldn't breathe in that van without being afraid some was going to happen. She said she prayed for your safe trip back to this church."

Jorrie looked at him in shock. He could not believe

that Mother Walker was taking a report on him all this time.

"She also told me about a dispute on the van." Rev. Dobson said. "All those sisters that have hope of being Mrs. Jorrie Keller."

"It really wasn't anything," Jorrie said and smiled.

Rev. Dobson smiled and said, "I know everything that goes on in the church. I tell you what. I know that you need a break from the van. So I'm going to let Deacon Mark drive for the next few Sundays."

Jorrie smiled, "Ok."

They shook on the deal and went their separate ways.

Three Sundays later, Jorrie return to the church. He was more cheerful than usual. He sat in his usual sit next to Rev. Dobson. Nobody heard from Jorrie in three weeks. The sisters of the church were beginning to worry about their dream man. This Sunday was going to be different from the other Sundays. Jorrie handed Monica, the woman that read the announcements, an envelope. She opens the envelope and her mouth flew open. She walked up to the podium and read the announcements. When she got to the envelope that Jorrie gave her, she took a deep breath and read the card to the congregation.

Mr. and Mrs. Theon Cobb would like
to announce the upcoming marriage of their daughter
Melissa Devonna Cobb
To
Jorrie Scott Keller
May 21, 2001
At St. Luke Baptist Church

Meagan looked at him in shock. Ethel excused herself to the restroom. The whole church started shouting amen and praises the Lord. Rev. Dobson was smiling. After church, it wasn't that many women standing outside to get on the van. It was enough just to make one trip. Meagan was standing outside waiting on Jamica. Ethel was in Deacon Mason's car crying. She had lost the love of her life. Jorrie got out of the van. Melissa got out of the green car and walked up to him. They kissed. Meagan glanced over there as she got into Jamica's car. They stop kissing.

"You know what," Jorrie said. "You made me the happiest man alive."

They got into the green car and left.

Endless Love

Adrian Hubert thought that she would never be here on her graduation day. She sat near a bed in St. Ellis Hospital praying that John will wake up and everything will be alright. The doctor came in the room. He walks up to the bed. He checked John. He wasn't breathing on his own since he came in. The doctor touched Adrian on the shoulder and asked her to come outside with him. Adrian got up and walks out the room door with the doctor.

The doctor turns to her. He wasn't smiling. He said, "We don't expect him to make it through the night."

A tear dropped down from Adrian's face. The man that she had planned to spend the rest of her life with is dying in front of her eyes.

"Is there anyone that you want us to call?" the doctor asked.

Adrian looked at the doctor and shook her head no. She went back into the room with John lying there in the bed. The oxygen was making his chest go up and down. He looks lifeless. She sat back down next to John. She thought about the first time she met John Hubert.

    Adrian was a freshman at Parks University. The dorm was too noisy. So she went to the library every night and study. She was writing on a paper. John was just getting out of a study group. He always passed by her at the same table but this time there was something different about her. He didn't know what. It caught his eye. Her long jet black hair was pulled back into a ponytail. He went to the front desk. His friend, Donna, was at the desk.

    "What do you want now?" Donna asked.

    "Now Donna," he said, "what make you think that I want something?"

    Donna gave him the eye and said, "You always want something."

    "Well," he said, "since you think I want something, what is that girls name sitting over there?"

    He pointed to Adrian, who had her head in a book.

Donna laughed softly. He was kind of offended by the giggle.

"Her name is Adrian," Donna answered. "She is not in your league."

"And why would you say that?"

"Now do you want me to go through the list?" Donna smiled.

"I don't know what you are talking about," John said.

"It was Candice last week" Donna implied.

"Ok. Ok. Ok," John said.

"All I'm saying is that she is too nice for you."

The library was about to close. Everyone was leaving. Adrian stayed at the table. John was walking toward the table that Adrian was sitting at. Donna grabbed his arms. John looked at her. She nodded her no. John snatched his arm back. He walked out the door.

The next night, John was back to the library. He was on a mission. He had every intention of talking to Adrian. He didn't know what it was but she was someone that he just had to get to know. He sat at the table across from her. Donna was too busy tonight to notice that he was there. He stayed at the library until it was about to close. Then he made his move. Adrian was getting stuff together to leave. John made his

move. He approached her table.

"Do you need any help?" John asked.

"No," she said, "thank you."

She continues to put her books in her book bag.

"My name is John Hubert," he said.

Adrian picked up the bag and walked out the door. John followed her. She sat on a bench in front of the library. John sat next to her.

"So what is your name?" he asked.

"Adrian," she answered.

"So, where are you from?"

"Here," she answered.

Donna came out the door. She saw that John had gotten to Adrian. She walks over to them.

"Are you ready to go back to the room?" Donna

asked.

"Do you have to go so soon?" John asked.

Donna grabbed Adrian by the arm and they started to walk off. John ran up behind them.

"Wait!" he shouted as he ran up behind them.

Adrian stopped. She waited for John to catch up with them. Donna frowned as John walked up to them.

"Let me help you with your book bag," John said as he took Adrian's book bag from her. Donna threw her bag at him. They walked. It was quiet at first. They didn't say anything on way back. When they made it to the dorm, John opens the door. Donna walked in and went to the lobby. Adrian stood in the door.

"I would like to thank you for walking us back to the dorm," she said.

She kissed John on the cheek. John blushed. Adrian walked in the lobby and joined Donna. John watched the two of them walk down the hall to the room. When he couldn't see them anymore, he left.

The next night, John went to the library. He saw

Adrian wasn't sitting at her usual table. She was sitting in the back of the library. It wasn't anyone back there but her. John walked over and took the sit next to her.

"Hello," John said.

Adrian looked up. She gave him a big smile. She was hoping that he would show up.

"Hello," she greeted him back.

"How was your day?" he asked.

"Good," Adrian replies. "And yours?"

"Fine," John said. "What is you major?"

"Journalism," she replied. "And yours?"

"Business accounting," he answered.

"You never told me where you were from," Adrian said.

"St. Louis," John replied.

They talked until the library closed. Then they both sat on a bench waiting on Donna to get off. They laugh and talked. When Donna walked out the library, she frowned at them. They look up and saw Donna standing there.

"Are you ready to go?" Donna asked in a sassy voice.

"Yes," Adrian answered. "John, will you walk with us?"

"Of course," John answered.

Donna sign as they started to walk to the dorm. John was carrying Adrian's book bag. They was talking and laughing as they walked. When they got to the dorm, John opens the door to the lobby of the dorm for the girls. Adrian walked in the lobby. Donna walked in a few seconds behind her. Donna said to John, "Don't break her heart." John smiled. Donna walked into the lobby. John walked back to the library. John has been walking Adrian and Donna to their dorm for about two weeks now. Donna, who did not approve, starts liking John walking with them at night.

One night, it was raining. The library was about to close and Donna was wondering how was they going to get back to their dorm. Neither Donna nor Adrian brought an umbrella. The library was closing when,

Adrian went up to Donna and asked how they was going to get back to the dorm. John came up and laughed.

"Why are you so worried?" John asked.

Donna and Adrian looked at John. They thought that he had lost his mind.

"It is raining," Adrian said. "We don't know how we are going to get back to the dorm?"

John laughed again and said, "I'm going to take you in my car."

Both the girls looked at him.

Adrian then said, "You are telling me that we could have been riding to the dorm all this time."

"Basically," John said. "But I enjoyed our walks."

Donna hit him on the arm. They went to a blue Chevy on the parking lot. John opens the door for the girls. They got in. He closed the door and ran to the driver's side of the car. He opens the door and quickly jumped in the car. They drove off. The radio was playing some old school music. Adrian started to sing. John smiled.

"Your voice is beautiful," John said.

"Thank you," Adrian said.

"I know this club that plays old school music and serve some good soul food," John said. "Would you like to go?"

Adrian smiled and replied, "When?"

"Saturday."

"Ok," Adrian answered.

John smiled. Donna was happy for them.

"We have to find you something to wear," Donna said.

They were at the dorm. John got out the car. He ran to the trunk to get his big red umbrella. He opens it up and closed the trunk. He went on the passenger side of the car and opens the door for Adrian and Donna. They got out the car and under the big umbrella. They walked to the door. John opens the door for them. Donna went in first. As John held the door for Adrian, she leaned over and kissed him on the cheek. John blushed. Adrian went into the lobby.

"See you on Saturday," Adrian said.

John smiled as Adrian walked away. As she walked off she blew him a kiss. John closed the lobby door. He got into the car and drove off.

It was Saturday. John had come early. He wanted to make sure that he was on time. He went into the lobby and walked to the front desk. The lady at the front desk was busy writing. John coughs to get the lady's attention. She looked up.

"May I help you," she said with an attitude.

"Yes," John said. "Will you call Adrian Baxter and tell her that her date is here?"

She looked John up and down. Then she picked up the phone and called Adrian.

"And your name is?" the lady asked.

"John Hubert," he said.

She hung up the phone and pointed to the lobby.

"Go have a sit in the lobby."

John went and sat down in the lobby. The other woman was looking and giggling at him. They acted like they haven't seen a man. Adrian walked into the lobby. She had on a black and purple dress with black pumps. Her jewelry was silver. She had silver studs in her ears. She had on a black jacket. She carried a purple clutch. She walked up to John. John stood up. He had never seen Adrian with her hair down.

"You look beautiful," John said.

"Thank you," she smiled. "You look handsome yourself."

"Thanks," he said. "Are you ready to go?"

"Yes."

John grabs Adrian's hand and escorted her to his car. When they got there John opens the door. Adrian got in and John closed the door. He walked over to his side and got into the car. Then they drove off to the restaurant. When they got there, John opens the car door for Adrian. He then opens the restaurant door for her. They went up the host and he sat them down near a window. John even pulled out her chair for her. The waiter came over promptly shortly after they were seated. He took their order. The waiter went and got their drinks. They talked while waiting for their food.

"What brought you to Park University?" Adrian asked.

"Well," John said, "My mother went here when she was my age. She told my sisters and me stories about her experience at the university. I want to see for myself."

"What did your mother get her degree in?"

"Education," John answered. "She is a counselor at Langston Middle School."

"Did your father go to college?" asked Adrian.

"No," he answered, "he was in the Army. He is a retired sergeant."

The waiter came back with their food. They ate and continued their conversation. Afterward, they got on the dance floor and dance. They slow dance on the song *Endless Love*. He held on to Adrian tight while they were dancing. It was getting late and he took Adrian back to the dorm. It was silent in the car. When they arrived back at the dorm, John got out of the car. He went to the passenger side of the car and opens the door. He assisted Adrian out of the car. After he closed the door, they held hands as they walk towards the dorm.

"I enjoyed this night with you," Adrian said.

John smiled and said, "Thank you."

"I would like to go out again," Adrian said. "Let's catch a movie next time."

"Sure," John said.

He opens the lobby door for Adrian. Adrian let go of his hand and walked into the lobby. Before she walked in the lobby, she kissed John on the lips. He let go of the door and wrapped his arms around her waist. As they were kissing, she didn't want to let him go. She pushed him away. John stood there in a daze. He opens the door again for Adrian. She walks in the lobby. John walks back to his car.

Adrian woke up sitting in the chair. She had dosed off for an hour. She looked up at John in hope that his condition had change. His eyes were still close. She took her hand and begins to touch him. She looked at her ring on her left hand. She starts having thoughts about the day she received the ring.

It all happens when John and Adrian had been dating for two years. It was the first of March. John was going to graduate in two months. He had decided on the first day of March that he would ask Adrian to marry him. He wanted to do it on Valentines but he couldn't bring himself to ask. Now he was brave enough to do it. He had saved his money from his internship this summer to buy her the ring.

On this day, he went to the class she was in. He always walked her from her classes. Adrian had just walked out of the class when John had got there.

"Hi there," she said.

She leans towards him and kissed John on the cheek. He took her book bag and hand. They started walking towards Adrian's dorm. It was half way to the dorm when John stops in front of the clock tower. He reached into his pocket and pulled out a black velvet box. He got down on one knee and opens the box.

"Adrian Nicole Baxter," he said, "will you marry me?"

Adrian smiled. She wasn't expecting him to ask her so soon. She shook her head yes. John took the ring out the box and put it on her ring finger. He got up off his knee. Adrian kissed him passionately.

"I love you," she told John.

"I love you too," John replied back.

They went to the library and told Donna. Donna hugged the both of them. Then they call their parents. Adrian's mother started planning the wedding that she thought her daughter should have. John's mother started planning a wedding too. It was days that they would argue because of their mothers. It was a week before spring break. They was sitting outside of the student union.

"I'm tired of us always arguing," John said. "Is this how it always going to be when we get married"

Adrian looked up at him and asked, "Do you love me?"

John looked into her eyes and can tell she was hurt from all this beggaring. She is still the woman that he wanted to spend the rest of his life with.

"Why don't we elope?" He asked.

"I think that that will be an excellent idea," Adrian replied.

"We can do it spring break," John said. "We can go up to the courthouse Friday. Then we can go to Hot Springs for a honeymoon."

"We can do that," Adrian said.

So the plan was set. After Adrian last class, they would go to the courthouse and get married. They knew that their parents would be furious but it was about what they wanted. They agree not to tell anyone.

Friday came. Adrian had a white dress that she had when she pledged last year. John came to get Adrian from class. She was wearing her white dress. She walked out the class room. John was standing outside the door. He smiled at Adrian. John grabbed Adrian book bag and hand. He escorted her to his car. They drove to the courthouse. They filled out the necessary papers and went toward a justice of the peace.

"Do you, John Lenard Hubert, take Adrian Nicole Baxter to be your lawfully wedded wife?" the justice asked.

"I do," John replied.

"Do you, Adrian Nicole Baxter, take John Lenard Hubert to be your lawfully wedded husband?"

"I do," Adrian replied.

"By the state of Arkansas," the justice said, "I pronounce you husband and wife. You may kiss the bride."

John kissed Adrian. Finally she was Mrs. John Hubert. After the ceremony, they went to Hot Springs.

The first two days they did not leave the room. The rest of their stay there, they toured the city and took pictures. On the last day, they went to church. They enjoyed the service. Afterward, they went back to the campus.

"I had a great time," Adrian said.

"We can have a great time at home too," John said.

When they got back to the campus, Adrian got her things and move in with John. They called their parents. John's parents was very disappointed, especially his mother. She was buying things for the wedding. Adrian's mother was furious at her. She could not believe that Adrian could do her like that. It was more about Mrs. Baxter than Adrian. But she got over it and congratulated them.

Adrian moved into John's apartment. They stay there. John graduated that May. He was offered jobs out of town but he did not want to leave Adrian. He wanted her to finish college. The best job that John could find was in Little Rock. And he drove back and forward every day. He did not want Adrian to work. He wanted her to focus on school. He didn't mind working. He knew when she graduated that they could leave Arkansas.

It was Adrian's graduation. John was called in to work. He tried to explain to his boss that he couldn't because his wife was going to graduate today. His boss didn't care. He said it was an emergency and needed to be dealt with right now. So he got up early that morning to go to work.

Adrian went to the graduation breakfast alone. She really was expecting to go with John but he couldn't make it. He said he would be there when she walk across the stage. As she was getting ready to go to the convention center, her phone rang.

"Hello," she said.

"Hi baby," John said. "How is everything going?"

"Fine," Adrian said. "I'm getting ready now."

"Well," John said, "I will be there soon. I'm wrapping this up at the office and about to get on the road."

"I'll see you when you get here," she said.

"I love you," John said.

"I love you too," she said back to him.

Adrian hung up the phone and continues to get ready. She goes to the convention center with her parents. John notices he had two hours before graduation. He told his boss he had to leave. His boss thanks him for coming in. He got on the road. He didn't call to tell Adrian that he was on his way. He was speeding. He was going ninety when he went into the curve. He lost control of the car and flipped into the mean. The car was upside down. Other cars stop to assist. They called the ambulance. All John was mumbling Adrian's name. When he got to the hospital, they work on him. They had to revive him twice. He wasn't breathing on his own. The nurse went through his clothes and found a cell phone. She called the last number he called, Adrian. Adrian mother answered the phone.

"Hello," Mrs. Baxter answered.

"Hello this is Maria at St. Ellis Memorial Hospital," the nurse said.

Mrs. Baxter knew that it wasn't good news. They

were at the convention center. Adrian was getting ready to line up to march in the arena. The nurse told Mrs. Baxter what had happened. Mrs. Baxter went and got Adrian out of the lineup.

"Mama," Adrian said, "what is wrong?"

"We need to go the hospital," Mrs. Baxter told her.

"Why?"

"I explain on the way," replied Mrs. Baxter.

They left the convention center. They drove to St. Ellis. Adrian ran to the desk. They called the ER. A doctor came out to talk to Adrian.

"Are you a relative to Mr. Hubert?" the doctor asked.

"I'm his wife," she said.

The doctor took a deep breath and said, "Mr. Hubert has been involved in a car accident. He sustains a traumatic brain injury. The injury caused edema. He is not breathing on his own. We gave him some meds to make him comfortable. We can't do anything until the swelling going down."

That was three weeks ago. Now it is time to say good bye. She sat there by his side and wouldn't move. His mom sat there with her. But tonight she just couldn't take it anymore. She went to the apartment to get some rest. Adrian sat there alone watching the love of her life die. He was squeezing her hand. At the last moment he let go. She knew it was time. She stood over his bed.

"I never imagine coming to this moment so soon," she said. "I love you some much. Good bye my love."

The monitor went off. She kissed him gently on his forehead and said, "You will always be my endless love."

Caught up

Marquelia Andies lives a simple life. She works at Lane and Associate Law Firm. She is one of the top attorneys in the state of Arkansas. She lives in a house in Douglas, a suburb of Trevor. She worked very hard to get where she is today. Just to think that this is the same little girl from Nutbush, Mississippi. People use to say that Marquelia wouldn't amount to nothing. The same bronze chubby little girl that was supposed to have five babies and live on the system like her older sisters and mother is more than what they thought she would be. Her goal in life was to put a kink in that chain. Marquelia Jefferson-Andies wasn't your normal woman.

Marquelia has a family. She has a loving husband that she meet while in law school. Michael own his owe detail shop. At that time he only had just one detail shop. Now he has four including one in Little Rock. He has a son that was five at time they met. She loved him so much that she called Malik, the son, her own. After Marquelia finished law school, she married Michael.

About three years later Marquelia was pregnant with their daughter, Mikki Neshay. Marquelia Andies has the perfect life.

    One day out the week is dedicated to the family. This night for the Andies is Saturdays. On this night the family usually goes out and eats. Afterward they would catch a movie or go bowling. This weekend, Michael had other plans. He told his wife that he had to do some paper work at the Little Rock store and would be home late. Marquelia got the kids together and they went to Jay's Pizza Parlor to eat. The kids were missing their father, so she decides to get the pizza to go and rent a movie. She went to the rental store and rented three movies. Then they went home.

    Marquelia walked in the door with Mikki sleep in her arms. Malik was carrying the pizza and movies. Marquelia went to Mikki's room to lay her down on Mikki's bed. She heard a noise. It sounds like a moan. Marquelia thought that her husband was gone. She cracked the bedroom door open. She couldn't believe what she saw. Her husband, Michael sitting on their bed let another woman suck his dick. Her hazel eyes widen with shock. She couldn't believe that her husband would do such a thing. Her world was shattering right before her eyes.

Marquelia still had Mikki in arms. She rushed to the den where Malik was playing his game.

"Come on," said Marquelia. "Let's go over Tara's house."

"But Mama," Malik winds.

"Don't but Mama me," Marquelia said with a sharp voice. "Go to the car."

Marquelia put Mikki in her car sit and drove over her friend, Tara Morris, house. When she came back to the house she went to through the back door coming in the kitchen. She got her foot stool out and looks in the cabinet just above the refrigerator. That is where she keeps her Smith & Wesson. She also had a pack of Blacks in there too. She took them both down. She lit the black up. She took a puff off it and put it in the ash tray. She went to the room. The door was cracked. She saw the woman on top of her husband. Marquelia open the door. She shot at the head board of the bed. The woman jump up. Marquelia's eyes widen as the short old woman jumped out the bed. The woman grabbed her clothes and ran out the room.

"How dare you!" Marquelia shouted.

Michael jumped up out the bed.

"Now baby it's not what you are thinking," he said.

"Not what I am thinking!" Marquelia shouted. "I can kill your ass right now and get away with it."

"It was an accident," Michael said.

"Accidentally slipped in her pussy," Marquelia said.

"I thought that all this shit was over with when we decided to get married. But I guess I was an ass to believe it."

Michael got out the bed in his bare nudeness. All you can see is his chocolate cut abs. Marquelia point the gun at him with the cigar in her mouth.

"Let's talk about this," Michael said.

"Action speaks louder than words," Marquelia said.

"Look," Michael said, "I love you. She is just a hoe helping you with my need."

Marquelia knew that Michael is a dumb ass. She put the gun to the side to take a puff off her cigar. She couldn't believe what came out of his mouth. To use their sex life as an excuse to sleep with another woman made her lose all trust in him. She walked out the room. She went to the kitchen and put the gun back above the refrigerator in the cabinet. Michael walked in the room with his blue satin boxers on. He walked up to Marquelia and hugged her. She pushes herself away.

"I think you should leave," Marquelia said.

"Marquelia, I love you," Michael said.

"But you never said that you're sorry."

Michael looked at her. Tears were flowing down Marquelia's caramel face. He couldn't stand to see

Marquelia cry.

"I think you should leave," Marquelia said again.

"Marquelia," Michael said, "I'm sorry. I need you. I can't live without you."

Marquelia walked out. She went to her room and packed up a bag with clothes. Michael walked in the room.

"Where are you going?" he asked.

"Away from you," she replied.

She closed the bag and walked out the door.

Marquelia came back to the house after two weeks of being gone. She would have gone back if she wouldn't have run out of clothes to wear. She opens the door to find her living room in chaos. She would have thought that he would at least pick up behind himself concerning that he is a neat freak. His shoes were left at the door. Anyone could have tripped over them. She picked them up and placed them to the side. She walks into the room where the deed was done. The headboard had been taking out and the mattress had been placed on the floor. It looked as if he had washed some of the clothes and didn't put them away. Marquelia looked around and started to clean up the room. She put up all the clothes. She looked at the bed and found the same sheets were on the bed. She stripped the bed. She put the linen in a trash bag and took it to the garbage. She came back in and started picking up in the front room. She put everything back in its place. She then went back into her room and took the mattress and box springs and dragged them to the corner. She then decides to go to the store and buy an air mattress. She got in her car and went to Wally World.

When Marquelia came back she saw a blue truck at the house. She parked behind it. She got out and opens up the trunk. She pulled the few bags from her trunk and went into the house. She opens the door to find Michael sitting on the couch. He was playing some old school r & b music in the background. He had a beer bottle in his hand. She walked passed him without speaking. She went in to the room and started putting up the things that she had bought. Michael walked in the room. He knew that she was hurting. He didn't want see her like that.

"I'm sorry," he said in a sad deep voice.

All Marquelia could do was look at him evilly. She kept on doing what she was doing. She took the queen size air mattress out the box. She took the pump and plugs it into the wall. Michael walked over to help her. She gave him another evil look. This look was deeper than the other. Michael step out of the way and let her continue to work.

"I'm going to pick up the kids," he said softly.

Marquelia kept on doing what she was doing. Michael walks out the room. He knew she needed room to get her frustrations out. He went outside. He got Mikki's car seat out of Marquelia's car. He threw it into his truck and drove off. When Michael came back with the kids, he could smell the aroma of his favorite meal, fried catfish and turnip greens. Malik ran into the house. He was glad to be at home after being over Tara's house. Malik had to sleep in one of Xander's twin bed. Michael picked up Mikki and walked in the house. Malik was in the kitchen mouthwatering for the catfish Marquelia was cooking. Michael took Mikki to her play pin. Marquelia was still cooking. Michael walked up behind her.

He said, "So you forgive me."

Marquelia smiles at him. She kept stirring the turnip greens. Michael kissed her on the neck. She stood in the same spot. She did not move. He then decides to set the table up for dinner. He asked Malik to help him. Marquelia started to prepare the meal for serving.

Later that night, the family sat down at table. To Michael, it seems like an average family dinner. There wasn't anything said while everyone ate their food. When they were finish, Michael cleared the table and Marquelia started to get Mikki ready for bed. After she put Mikki down, she went back to the kitchen. She opens the cabinet and grabbed a wine glass. She grabbed the footstool and went to the cabinet above the refrigerator to get the cigars that she had open two weeks ago. Michael looked at her as she climbs down. He thought that she was going to get the gun out. She grabs her wine glass and goes into the living room. She goes behind the bar and gets a bottle of wine. She turns on the CD player. Music started to play. She sat on the couch and lights her cigar. She poured herself a glass of wine. Michael walks in. He went to the behind the bar and got himself a beer. He sat beside here. Marquelia sat there and acted like he wasn't there.

"How was your day?" Michael asked as he took another sip of his beer.

Marquelia took another puff of her cigar and then she picked up the wine and turn up the glass. She didn't say anything to him. Michael scooted next to her and tried to cuddle with her. Marquelia pushed him away. She poured her another drink. He tried again. She threw the wine on him.

"You need to go find your old lady to cuddle up with," Marquelia said. "She is the one that supposes to be helping me out."

Michael looked at her in shock. He didn't believe what he had heard from her.

"It is you that I want," Michael said.

"No," she said, "you want that old bitch. So I must not be all that. So she can be the one that suck your dick and ride you like there is no tomorrow."

She got up. She picked up her glass. She took the cigar and put it out in the ash tray. She looked at Michael. He could she in her hazel eyes that she was hurt. He was still wondering what he can do to make it up to her. He really doesn't want to lose her. She is a good woman.

"By the way," Marquelia said, "you are sleeping in the guest room."

Michael frowned. He was hoping that he could hold her soft body tonight. He sat on the couch listening to the music.

"She will forgive me," he said to himself. "She always does."

He sat back and took another sip off his now warm beer. He looked at the time and went to bed.

Wedding Day

It was the morning of the wedding. KeKe was up bright and early as usual. She was kind of nervous about today. The man that she loved for two and a half years was going to be her husband. She had been daydreaming about this day for seven months now and it's finally here. She knew if she would just hang in there that everything would be alright. KeKe heard a knock at the door. She went to answer it. She looked about the window and saw no one was there. So she opens the door and looked around. She didn't see anyone. She thought that it was another trick that her sorrors was trying to play on her. But she looked down at her feet and saw a package. She bent down and picked it up. She saw her name on the package. She closed the door and went back to the kitchen.

She sat down at the table and opens the package. She pulled out a pair of black and gold underwear. She looked inside the underwear and saw *Property of 24 K-Kat.* Under it was his name, Golden prophet. She opens the letter and read it.

Dear Ta Keisha,

I have been messing around with your man for about a year now. And I thought you should know before you marry him. Every night after he leaves you, he comes around my way and spends the night. Just ask yourself, how he got that diamond stud in his left ear. I thought that you would like to know that I brought for him last year. Just to prove that I am telling the truth, I enclosed the underwear that you gave him for Christmas.

The letter wasn't sign. Tears started to drop from her eyes. How he dares sleep with another woman, she thought to herself. I gave this sorry ass nigga my heart and he wish to break the damm thing just before our wedding. She heard the back door open and she hides the envelope and the underwear. A high yellow short woman walked in. She had her shoes in hand. KeKe stuff the underwear and letter back into the envelop. The woman looked up and saw KeKe's chestnut brown eyes that were now red as the devil.

"What's wrong KeKe?" she asked.

"Just crying tears of joy," KeKe answered with a smile.

Two women, one about two inches shorter than the other, walked in the kitchen. They both had on yellow robs and lavender slippers. One of them was a caramel colored with long reddish brown hair. The shorter one was heavy with brown hair but she was heavy in all the right places. The shorter one walked up to KeKe and hugged her.

"What's wrong?" she asked

KeKe looked at the both of them and ran off. She went upstairs to her room. She lay in her bed crying with the door close. One of the short women ran upstairs behind her. She knocks on KeKe's door.

"Go away Zora!" KeKe shouted.

Zora did just that.

About three hours later, KeKe got up and decides to put on some clothes. She looked in her draw and got out her gold pullover with some lavender cutoff jeans.

She put that on with her lavender and gold Pike's. Then she pulled her long silky black hair into a ponytail. She picks up her cell phone and keys off the desk. She opens the door to her room and across the hall to Zora's room. She looks under Zora's bed to get a carton of cigarettes. She opens the carton. She only takes two packs. Then she takes Zora's cell phone off the charger and replaces it with hers. Their cell phone was identical. Zora wouldn't know the different. She walks out of Zora room. Then she went back to her room and gets two bags off her bed. She rushes out the house to the garage. She turns off the alarm on her '93 gold Accord. She opens the door and then throws the bags over in the front seat. She opens the garage door. KeKe hops into the car, starts it up and drove off. Zora saw her and thought that she was on her way to the church. She is going to marry that fool any way, Zora thought to herself.

    The ushers escorted Mrs. Martin and Mya to their seats. Mrs. Martin was carrying a gold bible. She was wearing a lavender chiffon dress trimmed at the bottom with lace of gold. Mya, KeKe's sister, was wearing a gold sequence dress trim in lavender at every opening. When they were seated, Mr. and Mrs. Glover walked down the aisle carrying the broom. Mrs. Glover, a woman that was the same age as Trevon, was wearing a low cut dress with specks of gold. Mr. Glover had on a tux with a gold bow tie and cummerbund. The flower girl litters the floor with lilacs. The ring bearer carried a lavender pillow trimmed with gold lace. On top of the pillow were the bands of gold. After the ring bearer reached the alter the instrumental version of *For You*, by Kenny. The maid started walking down the aisle.

    The first maid was Rachel who was escorted by Carmichael, Zora's little brother. He goes by the name Hakeem. The maids was wearing low cut dresses made out of chiffon trimmed at ever open with gold lama. The dresses looked like goddesses rob. The dress length touched the top of their shoes. They carried lilacs and had lilacs in their hair. The groom men was wearing black tux with a gold collarless shirt. Hakeem looked at Rachel and thought to himself, *Out of all the maids, I had to escort the whore.* Rachel looked at him and thought, *He hasn't hit on me. He must be gay.* Mesha was next. She was escorted by Devin. She had her hair pin up in a French roll that was becoming of her. She thought to herself, *I wonder when he is going to pop the question to me.* She looked at Devin and smiled. *I'm lucky to have a man like Devin.* Velma walked down the aisle with her new ex man, Sammie. She really didn't want him to touch her. She went down the aisle with a fake smile on her face. She did it just to look right for the camera. *I really don't want to be here with this asshole. If it wasn't for KeKe, I wouldn't have showed up,* she thought. *And I wanted to marry this asshole. He slept with my roommate. I wish he would drop dead.* Sammie turn his had took a glance her hurt face. He couldn't frown nor smile. He kept a straight face. He felt guilt about what he had done. He wishes that he could take it all back. He felt her pain. He asked himself, *What can I do to make it better?* Velma took her arm away from Sammie after they got to the altar. Shenise and Aaron were on their way down the aisle. Shenise was walking as if she was the bride herself. She was crazy about Aaron and he knew this. He told her that he wasn't ready for mind. The last maid, the maid of honor, was Zora. She was escorted by the best man, Torey. His suit was a golden yellow with a black collarless shirt. Zora looked radiant in her lavender tea length dress. Her dress was not trimmed in lama. It was plain but cute. To set off the dress she was wearing golden hoes that look like they came from the play *The Garden*. She carried a bouquet of lilac that had a gold ribbon tied around it. Torey looked at Zora and smiled. *I wonder where Tyree is, he thought to himself. Leaving a woman like Zora unprotected from the other men who want her. If Tyree wasn't my best friend, I would pick her up too. She needs to drop that zero and get with this hero. I know I can do all the things that Tyree can't do.*

    They got to the alter and the wedding march

begins. Everybody stood up and Mr. Martin was standing by himself at the door. He was expecting his daughter to join but she didn't. The pianist started the song over again. There was no KeKe. Everybody looked back expecting the bride to come out. Mr. Martin went to the room where KeKe was supposed to be. He knocked to be. He knocked on the door. There was no answer. He opens the door and saw KeKe wedding dress still on the chair. It looks as if it has never been touched.

    Mr. Martin went in the church to announce that the wedding has been called off. The guests looked at him in shock. Mrs. Martin walked towards Mr. Martin. Rachel went up to Trevon, who was still looking for his bride. Shenise, Velma, and Mesha were with Mrs. Glover trying to figure out where KeKe could be. Zora went to the room where the wedding dress laid. She remembers that the wedding dress wasn't there before. Then she heard her cell phone ring. She pulls it out of her purse and looked at the id. It was her number. She answered the phone wondering who it could be.

"Hello" she answered.

"Zorie," the voice said, "it's me, KeKe."

Zora was shocked.

"Where are you?"

"At the River Front," KeKe answered. "Are you alone?"

"Yes," Zora replied. "Why?"

"I got something to tell you."

KeKe told her why she wasn't here. She also told Zora what she had found on the door step.

"It is just a sick joke," Zora said.

"I don't think that this is a sick joke," KeKe said.

"I'm on my way to the River Front," Zora said.

"Please come alone," KeKe said.

"Ok."

Zora hung up the cell phone. She wanted to change. So she went home to change. But Zora didn't know that Deshun, a friend of KeKe, was outside the door listening to the conversation. If Zora knew, she would have gone to the River Front first. Deshun waited for Zora to leave the parker lot before he went to his car. He drove straight to the River Front.

When Deshun arrived at the River Front he saw KeKe sitting on the banks smoking a cigarette. She was holding a pair of black and gold underwear her hand. KeKe thought to herself, *How dare this bastard do this to me? I gave him two and half years of my life he goes off sleeping with a bitch. How could he!* Tears ran down her face. Deshun walked up and sat next to her. She looked at him and put out her cigarette. She threw the underwear into the river.

"What was that?" Deshun asked.

She looked at him and said, "Something that I should have done a long time ago."

Deshun put his arm around her for comfort. He had been waiting for this moment for a while. He knew that Trevon would mess up. She laid her head on his shoulder. Deshun remember the first day he saw KeKe. It was at freshman orientation '93. Deshun was the only student from Philadelphia. He felt kind of strange and alone in a new land like this. He was walking around looking for a friendly face to talk to. There he saw her. He saw a bronze vision of beauty. Her hair was cut extremely short but brought out her facial features. Her eyes were a soft brown. She wore a blue sun dress with brown saddles that was showing her blue painted toes. He fail l love with her at that moment. She was sitting with Torey and Sammie, two boys from her hometown. They were talking about how much they miss home when Deshun walked up to them.

"Where are you from?" he asked them.

The all looked at him and smiled.

"Chicago," KeKe replied. "Where are you from?"

"Philadelphia," Deshun replied.

They looked at him in shock. Someone from Philadelphia choose Park University. Deshun stared at KeKe.

"TaKeisha Martin," she said as she held out her hand to shake his. "And your name is…."

"Deshun Jackson," he replied.

They have been friends ever since. He always tried to get with her but it seem like someone would always step in the way. And now this happens. He was happy that Trevon cheated on her.

"Why didn't you show up for the wedding?" Deshun asked

She raised her head and asked him, "If you found your future wife in the bed with another man on the day of the wedding would you marry her?"

Deshun then understood where she was coming from. She looked at him with her brown eyes that were now red. She closed her eyes and moved toward him. She kissed him. At first he didn't want to kiss back but he did. He pulled back and KeKe open her eyes.

"Can we go someplace else?" KeKe asked.

"We can go to my place," Deshun answered.

"I'll follow you," she said.

Deshun got up. He helped KeKe get up. They both went to their cars and drove off. KeKe follows Deshun close behind.

Five minutes after they left, Zora pulls up. She looked for KeKe's car but did not see it. She walked around the River Front. KeKe was nowhere to be found. She took out the cell phone to call KeKe. There was no answer. Zora begin to get scared. She went back to her car and drove off. She started to think, *Where is KeKe?* She went back to the house to look for KeKe.

KeKe and Deshun arrive at the apartment. Deshun open the door and KeKe entered. He closed the door. KeKe took off her pullover. She was wearing a beige lace bra. She kicked off her shoes and socks. Deshun stood there in shock. Then she unbuttoned her cut off and pulled them off. He couldn't move an inch. He thought that he was dreaming. He always wondered how she would look naked. She walked up to him. She pulled off his black jacket. She threw it on the floor. KeKe started kissing him. She started removing his collarless shirt from his heated body. He helped her take of his pants by removing his shoes. He had on a pair of blue boxers with silver stripes. She pulled down Deshun's boxers. There was nothing between them but the skin between the two.

She pushed him onto the black leather couch. She leaned into his body and started to kiss him. He couldn't believe that this was happen right now. She started to lick him down to his bow of love. When she got to his bow of love, she started to lick it like a popsicle on a hot day. She got to the head and covered it with her mouth. She started sucking on it. Deshun's eyes rolled to the back of his head. He couldn't believe that this was happening. She stops and he pulled her up. He started to kiss on her. He laid her down on the couch. He started kissing her on her neck. He went from her neck to her right breast. He was a gentle as a man can be with her. He went all the way down to the river of love. He knew once you drink form this river there was no going back. But he knew what he was getting himself into.

He licked back up. He got up. He picked KeKe up and carried her in his strong arms to his bed room. He opens the door to the blue and silver room. The furniture was made of cherry wood. The bed set up high and had a silver bedspread on it. It had a lot of pillows that was blue. He laid her down on the bed. He reached into his night stand and grabbed a condom. He put it on his bow of love. "Deshun," KeKe called out softly. She spread her legs wide open. That made Deshun even harder. In KeKe's mind, she wanted to forget about the pain that Trevon had caused her. This was the medicine to make it better. Deshun started to push harder and she moan and groan louder. Deshun was hoping that the neighbors did not hear them. For the first time in a long time, Ta Keisha Martin felt loved.

    The next morning KeKe got up. She went into the living room and got the cell phone out of her pants pocket. She called Zora but did not get an answered. She left her a message. She put on her clothes. She looked for a piece of paper and a pen. When she found them, she wrote:

Thank you,

T

She went back into the room and put it on the night stand. She walked out the door. KeKe made sure the door was locked. She got into her car and drove off. About two hours later, Deshun woke up to find KeKe wasn't there. He got up and saw the note on the night stand. He got up and went to the bathroom to take a shower. He read it. He laid back into the bed.

"She'll be back," he said.

The Loner

Natosha Gregory has a daily routine. Weekdays Natosha gets up out the bed at five thirty and prepare herself for work. She would take a shower and then go to the kitchen. She turns on the coffee maker and brew herself a fresh cup of hazelnut coffee. She normally doesn't eat breakfast in the morning. Natosha goes to her room and dress for work. She makes sure that she leaves the house no later than half past six. She drives to Trevor Regional Medical Center listening to the gospel. She arrives there and goes to work until three. She goes across the street to the Wellness Center and work out for about an hour and a half. Then she goes home and put dinner on. She eats dinner while looking at the evening news. Then she gets up and takes a shower. After her shower, she usually talks on the phone or read a book. Natosha waits for her husband, Lamar, to call most of the time.

Sgt. Lamar Gregory is active duty in the army. He has to travel to different places for months at a time.

Most of the time he is comes home for a week or two and he is back on the road. They don't have any children together. This makes their lifestyle easier to maintain. They want to have kids but they felt it was best that they wait until Lamar's tour of Iraq. This is his second tour and plans on taking a leave for about a year. She missed him very much and prays that he comes home safe and in one piece.

    After her phone conversation, Natosha goes to bed. She sleeps on the right side of the bed with a big long pillow representing her husband. She found herself to go to sleep better with the pillow. And this was her weekly schedule.

    During the weekend she would go shopping for items to send to Iraq for Lamar. She would also clean the house and make her weekly phone call to her mother. Sometime she invites her girls, Tara and Marquelia. She doesn't like it when they bring their tribes to her house. She loves her godchildren but they always messing up something. They usually come by themselves. They know that Natosha house is not equipped for kids. They drink wine and conversant about old college days, currents events, and kids. Natosha like to hear about the kids but finds herself left out the conversation because she can't relate to them. But she listens and don't say anything.

On Sunday, Natosha gets up and turn on the TV to a gospel station. She then gets in the shower and get ready for church. She gets there by a quarter until eleven so she can get a good sit. She tries to make it to all the church events and programs. Sometimes she sings in the church choir when she is needed. She does the church announcements. She is a member of the mission society. Natosha is very active in church.

On the first Friday of each month, Natosha goes to Reeves Drug Store and pick up her medicine. She has known Mr. Joe for years. He owned this store before she was born. Her mother and grandmother went to the store when they lived in Trevor. So she trusts Mr. Joe with all her drug needs. This Friday was different.

Natosha went to get her normal prescription. She walked in the store and picked up a magazine. Then she went to the back to the pharmacy. "Hello Ms. Katty," Natosha greeted the clerk who is usually always at the counter. "Hello Tosha," Ms. Katty responded. She went back to the back to get Natosha's prescription. Ms. Katty then came back with a bag. She hand the bag to Natosha. Natosha looks into the bag and found that this is not the usual medicine that she gets. Ms. Katty already went back to the back and to get Mr. Joe. But Mr. Joe didn't come out. A younger man came out. He was coco brown with dreamy eyes. He stood a little taller than Mr. Joe. He wore a pair of blue jeans and a gray tee shirt. He had some black rim glasses on the tip of his nose. His hair was cut in a low fro. He walked up to Natosha.

"Is there a problem?" he asked in his baritone voice.

"Yes," Natosha replied, "There is a problem with my prescription. These are the generic version of the pills that I usually get. I don't get these pills."

The young man took the bag and looked the bottle.

"I don't see a mistake. By the way how do you know that this is the generic version of the pills that you use to get?" He asked.

Natosha looked at him crazy like he didn't see that she was in scrubs.

"I'm a register nurse. I know my pills."

"Your insurance plan doesn't cover the pills that you usually get," he said.

"Where is Mr. Joe?" Natosha asked.

"On vacation," he replied.

"Where is Chris?" Natosha asked.

"He has the day off."

"What is your name?" Natosha asked.

"I'm Mr. Reeve's younger son, Rodney."

Natosha looked at him. She wanted to grab him by his neck and choke him. But she maintains her composer.

"Mr. Joe usually let me pay the different," Natosha said.

Rodney took the bag to the back and refills the prescription. Five minutes later, Rodney came back with the bag. Ms. Katty checked out up the prescription. Rodney stood there as Natosha paid for it.

"You have a nice day," Rodney said.

Natosha grabbed the bag and walked out the store. Rodney looked at her as she walked out the store.

"I got to get to know her better," he said to himself.

He walked back to the back.

Baby Daddy's Drama

Samantha was in her beauty shop working. She was doing a client's hair. She looked up at the clock and saw that it was almost time to go get Samuel, her son. She didn't want to leave her client's hair half way done and she had another client waiting on her. So she went to the back. She pulled out her cell phone to call Undre, her baby daddy.

"Hello," a woman's voice said.

"May I speak to Undre?" Samantha asked.

"No, you may not," the woman said.

"Nona," Samantha said, "I really don't have time for your childish games. I need to speak to Undre right now."

"No," Nona said, "you cannot speak to Undre right now."

"Is he busy?" Samantha asked.

"No," Nona said. "I just don't want you talking to him."

By this time Samantha was furious. She was tired

of Nona's bull shit. "Well," Samantha said, "can you ask him if he will pick up Samuel from school today?"

"No, he will not pick up your bastard child," Nona said.

Samantha could not hold it any longer. She had to show this bitch where she was coming from.

"Listen here bitch," Samantha said. "Don't you every call my son a bastard. Second of all he was here before you came into the picture. Next time you call my son a bastard, I'm coming to kick your high yellow ass."

"Don't worry," Nona said. "I'm on my way to your house now to kick your ass."

"Come on," Samantha said. "I'll be there waiting on your ass."

Samantha hung up the phone and called Apria, her older sister. She told her about Nona meeting her at her house. Apria said she was on her way. Apria called Donnatella, their oldest sister, and told her about Nona. Donnatella said she was on her way.

Samantha rolled her client's hair. She put her

client under the drier. Then she asked Lisa, a stylist in her shop, to finish her client for her. She hopped in her black Mustang and drove off. When she got to the house, Donnatella was sitting in her blue Cadillac waiting for her. Samantha looked under her seat and got out her glock 22. She put it in her purse. She got out the car. Donnatella got out hers. She was wearing her brown stiletto boots with blue jeans and a gold satin blouse. She looked as if she just came from work. She walked up to Samantha and gave her a hug.

"We are going to get this bitch today," Donnatella said. "You don't call my little nephew a bastard and think that you are going to get away with it."

They sat outside waiting for Nona to pull up. Apria pulled up five minute later. Apria knew they were prepared to beat Nona's ass outside. She got out of her car with a bottle of Merlot red wine.

Apria walked up to the two of them and said, "You don't want the neighbors thinking something about to go down. Let's go into the house and do this."

Donnatella and Samantha agreed with Apria and went in the house. Apria and Donnatella sat down in the living room. Samantha went into the kitchen and return with flute wine glass and a cork screw. She gave the cork screw to Apria to opens the wine. Then she poured it into the three glasses. They all were sitting there drinking.

"What possessed her to call Sammy a bastard?" Apria asked.

"Because she is a silly bitch," Donnatella said. "I told Undre to leave that dumb ass broad alone."

Samantha said, "She knows that she doesn't have his heart. That is what she wants."

There was a knock on the door. Samantha and Donnatella pulled out their glock.

"Put that shit up," Apria said.

They put the guns back in their purses. Apria unlocked the door and sat back down.

"It is open," Apria shouted.

A tall high yellow woman walked in wearing jeans

and a t shirt tucked in. She had on her white tennis that looked like they were a couple of years old. She saw Donnatella sitting on the couch and Apria in the chair by the door. Samantha was sitting on a stool.

"What the hell you want," Donnatella asked.

Nona took two steps toward Samantha. Donnatella scooted closed to the edge of her sit.

"She came to whoop my ass," Samantha said.

"Is that true?" Apria asked.

Nona didn't say anything. She rushes towards Samantha. Donnatella stuck her leg out and tripped Nona. Nona fell flat on her face. Nona got up. Apria got out of her seat and pushed Nona back down. Samantha went into her purse and pulled out her gun. She walked toward her and pointed the gun at Nona. Nona tried to get up but Donnatella got up and put her stiletto hill to Nona's neck.

"Now what made you think that I was going to let you whoop my ass," Samantha asked. "I called for Undre, not you."

Donnatella remove her heel from Nona's throat.

"You are still mess around with him," Nona said.

Donnatella and Samantha laughed.

"You are the only one that wants him," Donnatella said.

"If I wanted Undre, he wouldn't be with you," Samantha said. "The only time I talk to Undre is when Samuel needs something."

Nona rose up. She got back on her feet. Samantha put her gun down to her side.

"Next time you walked through this door trying to beat someone ass, you better bring an army because we going to whoop your ass," Donnatella said.

"It will not be a next time," Apria said. "Is that right Nona?"

Nona shook her head yes.

"Now get the fuck out of my house and don't come back," Samantha said.

Nona walked out the door like she had a tail between her legs. The three women looked outside as she got into her car. They notice that she got in the car on the passenger side. Donnatella looked and saw Undre on the driver's side. He was smiling. The car pulled off. They went back to drinking their wine.

Halloween Massacre

October 31, 1975

  After being married to Michael Peterson for the last three years, Charmaine was finally free. She was free to love who she wanted. This union wasn't one that was wanted. She only married him to regain her father's love. He wanted them to be together ever since they were in junior high. She never loved Michael and she told her father this several times. When she graduated from high school, she went to Chicago against her father wishes to attend Victory University. Her father shuns her from the family.

  While at Victory University, she major in music. It was her heart and soul. She had plans to be famous one day. Her best friends, Paula and Angelia, attended the university with their dreams too. A semester later, Charlie, Charmaine's brother, came. They were one big happy family. One day, Charmaine saw a flyer for a talent show. She talked Angelia and Paula into creating a girl group called Chi Divas. They entered the talent show. They didn't win but Charlie introduces them to Rome LaRue. He owned a recording studio named after him. He asked the girls do they want to record deal. They said yes and their careers took off.

By the spring of their sophomore year in college, they had a record playing on the radio. Rome insisted that they go on the road. It will only be during the summer and they would be back in time to register for the fall. They agreed to open up for other acts. It gave them more experience. Rome and Charlie went on the road them. This was kind of unusual for Rome to do but he wanted to make sure that no funny business went down. While on the road, he got better acquaint with Charmaine. They begin to date. When the tour was over, Charmaine went back to school. Rome continue to see her every chance he could. He had roses sent to her dorm room and would treat her and her friends out to dinner. By her senior year of college, Rome and Charmaine were exclusive. Rome had intentions of marrying her. He knew that she was the one.

That same fall of Charmaine's last year of college, Michael decide to come to Chicago. He was said to be sowing his oats, but he had another agenda on his mind. It was to try to woo Angelia to be his wife. But Angelia was engaged to Charlie at this time. He did everything he could to ruin their relationship. When he figures out that Angie was moving, he focused his attention to Charmaine. . Charmaine and Rome were having relations.

Charmaine graduated the spring of 1972. She went to presume her music career. But she had one problem. That same year in November, she discovers that she was pregnant with Rome's baby. She was debating whether to tell him or not. She thought about having an abortion. This is not supposed to happen now, she said to herself at night. She told Rome, who already knew, a month later. He was happy. By August of 1973, Charmaine gave birth to their son, Romeo. They weren't on good turns after she had Romeo, but she still loved him. They separated when Romeo was only two months.

Charmaine stayed with her grandmother, Anny, in Cherry Hill, just right outside of Chicago. Rome continued to stay on the north side of Chicago. He came to see Romeo and Charmaine when he could. Charmaine's grandmother kept Romeo while Charmaine would go to Chicago to record. Angelia and Paula wanted to quit the group to started families of their own. Paula married her college sweetheart, Patrick Torres. Angelia married Charlie. They both wanted families and careers of their own. Singing was Charmaine thing. That's when Rome suggested that Charmaine has a solo career. Rome got her backup singers and a band. Charmaine would come in the studio four times a week recording material for her debut album.

    In between all this time, Michael and June, Charmaine's oldest brother, came to visit. Michael was in the ministry and wants to become a pastor. June suggested it might be a good idea for him to ask Charmaine to marry him (even though it wasn't his first choice). June told her that by marrying Michael, she will regain her father's love. So they was engaged one day and married within a month. Michael had a church in Atlanta. Rome was furious. He refuses to let his son go live with a snake like Michael. He said he would keep him in Chicago. He moved Grandma Anny with him. Charmaine put her music career on hold to serve as the first lady of the church.

    Rome found companionship is a young lady name Jill Watson. She was his rebound girl and she wanted to be with him. His mind was there but his heart was still with Charmaine. She went back to Chicago once every two months to go see Romeo. One time Rome and Charmaine rekindled a moment. She realized how much she missed and loved him. It was a onetime thing and she went back to Atlanta. Two months later she was pregnant again with her daughter, Charlene. Rome swore that Charlene was his child. But Charmaine insisted that she was Michael's. Rome kept quiet about it. He didn't want to startle Jill.

One Saturday morning, Charmaine woke up to an empty bed. Her husband was already gone. She knew he open up the church on Saturday mornings for mission pray and cleaning. She wanted to talk to him about finishing her record. She got up and ready to go to the church. She got Charlene ready to see her dad. They got into the car and drove to the church. Charmaine got out of the car. She was carrying Charlene on her hip. She came to the front door and notice it was locked. She thought that he must be in his study. So she went to the side door and it was open. She went in and heard moaning sounds. It was coming from the sanctuary. She opened the doors, and the sound got louder. She walked to the pupil pit. Her eyes widen. She couldn't believe what she saw. Her husband was having sex with one of the sisters from their congregation. The sister opened her eyes and screamed. Charmaine ran out the church. She got in the car and drove back home.

    She packed Charlene and her clothes and went to Paula's house to stay. She needed time to think about what to do next. She stopped showing up at church. June came to Atlanta to talk Charmaine into going back to Michael. She told him that it would be a cold day in hell before she goes back. Then he mentions the respect that she was getting from their father. She told him that he would respect her even more if she left. Michael even came over a couple of times. Charmaine would call the police on him. She didn't want to see him anymore. She decided that she would move back to Chicago.

Now she is on a plane with Charlene, going back to Chicago. She knew that she should have never left Chicago. Her heart was there. She really didn't need the approval of others to live her life as she pleases. Chicago is home for her. She wanted to raise her kids there and pray that they love Chicago just as much as she does.

When she first came back, Rome treated her harsh. His heart was broken when Charmaine married Michael. He wasn't going to welcome her back with open arms. He wanted her to earn his love back. He was with Jill now. Well, he was with her physical but not mentally. It was days that Jill would get on his nerves. When Charmaine came back, Jill became jealous. But Rome did not make it any better. He started not coming around Jill as much. He would spend all day in the studio with Charmaine. Jill confronted him with this issue. He decided to make Jill a backup singer. That way he could spend more time with her. But that didn't work out as plan. She couldn't sing. So he gave Jill studio time. Eventually, Rome broke up with Jill. Jill became obsessed. She said that she will never let him go.

  It was Halloween night. Charmaine went back to Atlanta to finalize her divorce from Michael. She was flying back the same night to sing at the annual Halloween Party. This was her first solo performance. She was use to Angelia and Paula being on stage with her. Rome was making sure that there was extra security at this event. Jill has been threatening Charmaine and her family. She even went as far as trying to kidnap Romeo. Rome had told Charmaine to call him as soon as she gets to the airport. When Charmaine departed the plane, she went to a pay phone to call Rome.

"Hello," the tired deep voice said.

"Hello baby," Charmaine said.

Rome voice perked up, "Are you are the airport?"

"Yes," Charmaine said. "I'm going to take a cab to the hotel and get ready for the party from there."

"I'm going to send Henry over there to get you in an hour," Rome said.

"I'll be waiting," Charmaine said.

"Be careful," Rome said.

"I will," Charmaine said and she hung up the phone.

Charmaine got into cab and went to the hotel. Rome was upstairs his office. He was working on some last minute paper work. The Halloween party was going on down stairs. He was already in his costume. He had planned to go straight to the party after he finished. He has security all over the build. He was busy at work when he was startle by Melvin, his head security guard. Rome was working so hard he had not realized that

Melvin had walked in.

"Is everything alright Mr. LaRue?" Melvin asked.

Rome looked up and shook his head yes. Melvin walked out and patrol the building and Rome continue to work.

Five minutes later, Rome heard some gun shots. Then someone fall on the floor. Before he could open his drawer to get his gun, the door opens. A gun shot was fired. It hit his shoulder. Rome fell back on the floor. A tall slender woman dressed in a witch's costume walked towards him with a gun. Rome tried to get up. The woman shot him again in the leg.

"You're not going anywhere," the woman said.

She stood above him with the gun point at him.

"You hurt me, Rome," Jill said. "You hurt me bad."

She shot him again in his other leg.

"You just had to have you some Charmaine. I loved you. I wanted to give you a child. But you wouldn't touch me. You just had to go after her even though she married another man. You still had to have her. I wanted to marry you. I want us to spend the rest of our lives together."

She aimed the gun at his chest.

"I'm going to hurt you where you hurt me," Jill said.

She shot him one time in the chest. Blood started gushing from everywhere. She walked out with a smile on her face.

Charmaine arrived at the studio ready to perform. She walked in the doors of the build. She felt like something just wasn't right. She then went upstairs to Rome's office. She walked down the hall and saw someone lying on the floor. As she walked closer, she screamed. She ran in Rome's office to call the police. She reached for the telephone and saw Rome behind the desk. She called the ambulance and the police. They police got there first. They pronounced both of the victims dead on the scene. They questioned Charmaine. She told them about Jill threats. The she asked could she call home. When she called home she could not get an answer, she was scared. She ran down stairs. She bumped into Charlie and Angelia. She told Charlie there was no answer at her grandmother's. They all got into Charlie's car and drove off.

When they arrived at Grandma Anny's house, they found her on the floor unconscious. Charlie rushed to assist his grandma. Charmaine went to the phone to call the police. Angie went in search for the kids. She went into a room. She heard some whining coming from the closet. She opened the closet and saw Ashley holding Charlene in her arms. Tears were running down her face. Angie reached out and picked up Charlene, who was sleeping. She put her down on the bed. She went back to assist Ashley out the closet.

"She has Romeo," Ashley said.

"Who is she?" Angie asked.

Ashley paused for a minute to catch her breath and said, "Jill."

Angie and Ashley went into the living room with the rest of the family. Grandma Anny was waked on the couch.

She was explaining to Charlie and Charmaine what had happen. The police arrived shortly after. They took Grandma Anny and Ashley statements. An APB was put out for Jill and Romeo.

Charmaine beings to think it was all her fault. She thought about how she shouldn't have married Michael. She was in love with Rome. Now she couldn't tell him that she loved him. If she would have stayed and married Rome, Romeo would have been safe and Rome would not be dead. She got on her knees and started to pray.

"God please bring our little boy home safe," she said.

There was a knock on the door. Charmaine got up and opened the door. It was a police officer. He was holding a little boy dressed up as Dracula. Charmaine grabbed the little boy and hugged him. The police officer smiled.

"We found him at the bus station with a young lady," the police officer said. "When questioned, she tried to run and we caught Jill."

Tears streamed down Charmaine's face. She was happy to see her son. She hugged so tightly.

"I'm never going to let you out of my sight again," she whispered in his ear. "Mommy loves you."

"Love you," Romeo said.

Charmaine couldn't do anything. She gave him a kiss on the cheek and went in the house with the rest of the family.

Cleopatra Kaine is a native of Pine Bluff, Arkansas. She attended the University of Arkansas at Pine Bluff. She is a devoted mother. She has a passion for writing. She has written several books which include The Purple Book, Confession and Food for Thought: Thoughts of a Diva. She created a children series of books name Simply Delanie to address the daily issue that a child may face. She wrote Popular Bully and Boys are Icky, the first two books of the series.

Confession

Made in the USA
Charleston, SC
17 July 2016